D0041991

THE *DIARY OF A WIMPY KID* SERIES

1 *Diary of a Wimpy Kid*
2 *Rodrick Rules*
3 *The Last Straw*
4 *Dog Days*
5 *The Ugly Truth*
6 *Cabin Fever*
7 *The Third Wheel*
8 *Hard Luck*
9 *The Long Haul*
10 *Old School*
11 *Double Down*
12 *The Getaway*
13 *The Meltdown*
14 *Wrecking Ball*
15 *The Deep End*

MORE FROM THE *WIMPY* WORLD

The Wimpy Kid Do-It-Yourself Book

The Wimpy Kid Movie Diary

The Wimpy Kid Movie Diary: The Next Chapter

Diary of an Awesome Friendly Kid: Rowley Jefferson's Journal

Rowley Jefferson's Awesome Friendly Adventure

DIARY of a Wimpy Kid

THE DEEP END

by Jeff Kinney

AMULET BOOKS

New York

Cataloging-in-Publication Data has been applied for and may be obtained from the Library of Congress.

ISBN: 978-1-4197-4868-4

Book design by Jeff Kinney
Cover design by Jeff Kinney and Marcie Lawrence

Published in 2020 by Amulet Books, an imprint of ABRAMS.

Printed and bound in U.S.A.
10 9 8 7 6 5 4 3 2 1

ABRAMS The Art of Books
195 Broadway, New York, NY 10007
abramsbooks.com

TO RYAN

AUGUST

Thursday

I love my family and all, but I don't need to spend twenty-four hours a day with them, seven days a week. And that's EXACTLY the way it's been around here lately.

It's not just ME who's getting tired of this, either. We're ALL going a little nuts, and if things don't change soon, I think we're gonna go off the deep end.

Mom says we've been cooped up for too long, and we just need a vacation. But what we really need is a vacation from each OTHER.

That's not gonna happen anytime soon, though, because we don't have any MONEY. And the reason we don't is kind of a long story.

We've been living in Gramma's basement for two months, and I don't know how much longer we can keep going like this. Mom says that one day we'll look back on this time and smile, but she's not the one who has to share a futon with RODRICK every night.

The crazy thing is, Gramma's got plenty of room in her house, so I don't understand why our whole family has to stay in her basement. When we first got here, I called dibs on the guest room, but Gramma said it was already taken.

I don't think Gramma's too thrilled we're living with her, because whenever her friends come over she asks us to stay out of sight.

And that's kind of inconvenient since there isn't a bathroom in the basement, and her friends always stay FOREVER.

We can't use the kitchen when Gramma's got guests, which means we can't eat dinner until after they're gone. But last night I guess Rodrick got sick of waiting, so he heated up some leftover pizza in Gramma's dryer.

There's no TV in Gramma's basement, so the only thing we've got to entertain ourselves with is each OTHER. And believe me, that's not enough.

Mom says being bored is good, because it makes you use your imagination. But whenever I try it, I always end up imagining the exact same thing.

Something that's making the situation a lot harder is that Dad is working from home this summer, which means he's always around. And whenever Dad has a meeting, the rest of us have to pretend we're not there.

But that's not always easy to do, especially when you've got a three-year-old in the family.

Most of the time I just try to keep myself busy. Gramma's got stacks of puzzles down in the basement, and I've done a few of them by myself. But Mom always lets Manny put in the last piece to make him feel important.

If you ask me, I don't think Mom's doing Manny any favors by BABYING him. And it's gotten a lot worse since we started living at Gramma's.

Sometimes, after dinner, we'll play a board game as a family. But Manny can't handle complicated rules, so we always end up playing a game that doesn't require any SKILL.

We have to go to bed before it's even dark outside, because we're all on MANNY'S schedule.

These days, Manny's favorite bedtime story is a Noah's Ark picture book. It's about this guy who hears it's gonna rain for a really long time, so he builds a giant boat to ride out the storm with a bunch of animals.

The illustrations in Manny's book are all cartoons, and they make it look like a flood that wiped out half the Earth was kind of FUN.

But I guess if the drawings were more realistic, parents wouldn't buy it for their preschoolers.

I've got some questions about the Noah's Ark story, though. For starters, I wanna know why Noah let venomous creatures like snakes and scorpions on board. Because if it was ME, I would've used the opportunity to leave a few of those guys BEHIND.

And then I would've used the extra space for more of the GOOD animals, like puppies and hedgehogs and those pygmy hippopotamuses.

Luckily, Noah didn't have to make room on board for whales and fish, because they would've taken up a TON of space. And they probably didn't even know the flood was happening to begin with.

But it doesn't make a lot of sense that Noah let BIRDS on the ark, since they could've just FLOWN. And I bet he regretted that decision right away.

You only hear about the animals that SURVIVED the flood. But sometimes I wonder if there were some cool animals that DIDN'T make it onto the boat.

The way the story goes, after it rained for forty days and forty nights, it took 150 days for the floodwater to go back down. That means Noah was stuck on the boat with a bunch of animals, plus his wife and three sons.

And whenever I feel sorry for myself living in Gramma's basement with my family, I think about Noah and it makes me feel a little better.

Mom keeps saying she's glad we're all together right now, because she feels like time has slowed down. I've noticed that, too, but for ME it's not a GOOD thing.

Something that's making this summer feel really long is that I can't go to my friend Rowley's house. And that's because he's off on some big European vacation with his family.

When Rowley first told me about his family's plans, I tried to see if his parents might let me tag along. But I guess Mr. and Mrs. Jefferson aren't as sharp as I thought they were, because they never picked up on any of my hints.

So now Rowley's probably off having the time of his life while I'm doing five-hundred-piece puzzles in my grandmother's basement.

I think Mom feels bad we can't afford to do something special this summer, so she's been trying to make up for it.

She says we can go anywhere we want if we just use our imaginations. But to be honest, that's not really doing it for me anymore.

I think Mom's finally had enough, too, because last night she called a "family meeting" after dinner to brainstorm ideas for vacations that we can afford. But the problem is, everyone's got their OWN idea of a good time.

Dad wants to drive around and visit a bunch of Civil War battlefields and take part in a reenactment. But nobody else was crazy about putting on wool underwear in the middle of August.

Manny wants to go to the Animal Safari, which we used to visit a lot when I was little. But the animals in that place always seem so SAD, especially the donkey they painted to look like a zebra.

Mom said we could save money by staying close to home and visiting places in our own community. But I've gone on enough school field trips to feel like I know this town inside and out.

The only ones who could agree on what we should do were me and Rodrick. We both voted to go to the Thrills and Spills amusement park, which would be CHEAP since Gramma got half-price coupons in the mail.

Plus, they just opened a new roller coaster called Trackjumper that's supposed to be totally INSANE.

Mom said the rides at Thrills and Spills are too scary for Manny, so she suggested we go to Storybook Village, which has rides for all ages. But me and Rodrick have had enough of Little Miss Muffet's Mild Ride for one lifetime.

Since my family couldn't settle on anything, I suggested we all go on our OWN vacations and do a slideshow of everyone's trips when we get back.

Mom said the whole point of being on a family vacation is to do things TOGETHER. She says that one day us kids are gonna go our separate ways, and time's running out to make happy memories as a FAMILY.

But believe me, for THIS family to make happy memories together, it's gonna take a MIRACLE.

Monday

We finally figured out a way we could afford to go on a family vacation this summer.

On Saturday night, my great grandmother Gammie called Dad and asked if he could get rid of Uncle Gary's camper, which has been parked in her driveway for the past two years.

Apparently, Uncle Gary ran off to work as a rodeo clown, and she doesn't think he's coming back anytime soon.

At first Dad was MAD, because he's always cleaning up Uncle Gary's messes. But Mom said the camper was the solution to our vacation problems.

Mom said the reason vacations are so expensive is because staying in hotels and eating at restaurants cost a lot of money. She said the camper would take care of BOTH of those things.

Then DAD started getting excited. He said we could hit the open road and stop for the night whenever we FELT like it, and we could cook for ourselves, too.

All I know is me and my brothers were so happy for the chance to get out of Gramma's basement that we probably would've agreed to ANYTHING.

Mom says we'll have a lot of adventures along the way, and now I'M getting kind of excited about this trip, too.

In fact, I'm actually starting to feel a little bad for ROWLEY. Because while he's stuck in a boring museum on the other side of the world, I'm gonna be off doing something really WILD.

For the past two days, we've been getting ready for our vacation. And I'm a little worried that Mom's hoping to turn this into an educational trip.

But believe me, the LAST thing I'm planning on doing is any LEARNING.

Wednesday

This morning, we went to the grocery store and stocked up on food for the trip. Then we went to the camping superstore to get everything ELSE we're gonna need.

I was pretty excited, because we've never actually BOUGHT anything at the camping store before. Dad used to take me and Rodrick there when we were little, but that was just to kill time on a Saturday morning.

When we got to the store today, Dad went around and picked up some basic supplies, like lanterns and canteens and camping chairs.

But I went straight to the section of the store with the high-end gear. Because I figure if we're really doing this thing, I'm gonna want to be COMFORTABLE.

I picked out an inflatable pull-out sofa and hiking boots with little fans built into the heels, plus a solar-powered blender that can make a cherry slushie in thirty seconds.

Dad said those things weren't for SERIOUS campers, though, and made me put them back.

Dad said we're gonna "live off the land" as much as possible on this trip, and he picked out a few fishing poles. Well, I don't know about anyone else, but the only fish I'll eat comes in the shape of a STICK.

Manny and Rodrick got really excited about the idea of catching our own food, so they went off to find their OWN gear.

But Mom stopped them before they could get too carried away.

Rodrick was pretty disappointed. I guess he was planning on doing some trophy hunting while we were on our trip, and was hoping to decorate the kitchen when our house is finished.

After Dad was done shopping, he was ready to check out. But I think Mom was nervous that we weren't getting the right kind of equipment, so she asked a salesclerk to look over our stuff and see if we had everything we needed.

Well, this guy must've been a wilderness survival expert or something, because he had a LOT to say. And none of it made me feel confident about going on a camping trip.

The clerk said the number one thing we needed to worry about was BEARS, because there are a ton of them in the places we were going. But he said there were a few things we could do to protect ourselves, just in case.

The clerk said the first thing we needed to remember was to always tie up our trash and hang it in a tree so it would be out of reach for bears. Then he said if we REALLY wanted to be safe, we should buy a jug of wolf urine and spray it around our camp every night, because it scares bears off.

I tried to imagine whose job it is to COLLECT wolf urine, and I promised myself I'd start getting better grades in school so it doesn't end up being ME.

The clerk said the other thing we had to worry about was bugs like mosquitoes and ticks, so we should always put on plenty of bug spray.

I was totally on board with THAT idea, because one time Albert Sandy told everyone at our lunch table about this kid who fell asleep outside and got sucked DRY by a mosquito. And that sounds like a pretty bad way to go to me.

I was starting to get a little nervous when the clerk told us everything ELSE we needed. He said we had to have a first aid kit in case someone got injured, and waterproof matches in case our gear got wet.

Plus, we needed a compass if we got lost, a snakebite kit if someone got bit, and a flare gun if things REALLY got bad.

By the time we checked out, I was a little shook up. And I have to admit, Gramma's basement didn't seem so TERRIBLE anymore.

I think the guy at the camping store stressed Dad out, because after we paid for all the stuff, we kind of rushed out of there. And we were halfway home before realizing Rodrick was missing, and we had to go BACK.

After that, we drove to Gammie's house to pick up Uncle Gary's camper. I guess Dad had thought it was pretty much ready to go, but it was a total MESS inside.

I remember Dad telling me that when Uncle Gary got his first car, he used to keep a bunch of garbage inside so no one would STEAL it. Well, I think Uncle Gary had the same idea when it came to his camper.

We spent the whole afternoon cleaning it out, and I wouldn't have been too surprised if we'd actually found Uncle Gary buried somewhere underneath all that trash.

Once we got the junk out of there, we were finally able to take a good look around the camper. I could see how Uncle Gary was able to live in there for two years, because it had everything a person could NEED.

There was a stove, a sink, a kitchen table, and a little refrigerator. Plus, there was a bathroom with a shower in it, and some extra space above the cabin for sleeping.

We scrubbed everything down, but each time we thought we were finished cleaning, we'd find something else Uncle Gary had left behind.

And I don't mean to be rude or anything, but I seriously hope Uncle Gary has bought new underwear since he moved out.

After Gammie gave us some sandwiches to take with us, we hit the road.

When we started off, Dad was SUPER excited about the camper. He said since he could work anywhere he wanted now, we could live on the road until our house was finished, and maybe even LONGER.

Then Mom chimed in. She said we could travel around the country and record our adventures, then become one of those families who gets famous on the Internet.

I was actually starting to get into the whole RV lifestyle, too.

Mostly I just thought it was cool that I could use the toilet while we were cruising down the highway.

The only thing I didn't like about Uncle Gary's camper was that it didn't have seat belts in the living area, which was a problem whenever Dad hit the brakes.

When traffic slowed down, Mom let Manny sit in the front seat so he could feel like he was "driving." But I think she realized it was a mistake when he started laying into the horn.

It was cool being out on the open road and all, but after a while everything started to kind of look the same. So me and Rodrick went on our gadgets to pass the time.

After an hour or so, Mom said we'd had enough screen time for the day and we needed to be off our electronics.

Usually when Mom tells us we've had enough screen time, we'll take a break. But as soon as she stops paying attention, we'll get right back on. And after a while she'll get tired of fighting us and just give up, which is what we thought would happen today.

It turned out Mom wasn't messing around on this trip. When we got back on our devices, she put them in a clear plastic box that had a timer on top.

The second I saw that thing I knew what it was, because I'd seen the ads in one of Mom's parenting magazines.

Mom set the timer for two hours, then went back to her seat up front. Whoever made that thing knew what they were doing, because me and Rodrick couldn't figure out how to crack it.

Mom handed us some activities she'd created for the trip and said they should keep us busy for a while. But it wasn't that much fun playing Wildlife Bingo when we couldn't even identify half the animals we saw along the side of the road.

After another hour or two of driving, Mom and Dad started looking for places to stop.

There were some signs for "scenic attractions," so Dad pulled over at the exit for a place called Culpepper's Ravine.

Mom got all excited because she said we were like explorers who were about to see something new. But unfortunately, some OTHER explorers beat us to it.

We couldn't find any parking, so we had to move along. And it was the exact same story for the next three places we tried to stop.

I know I should feel lucky to be alive at a time when there's modern medicine and smartwatches and peanut butter-filled pretzels. But sometimes I wish I was born a little SOONER so I had a chance to actually DISCOVER something.

Because when you find something new, they NAME it after you.

But by now, everything worth finding has already been discovered.

And you wouldn't really want your name on any of the stuff that's left over.

GREG'S
DITCH

One time the planetarium in our town had a fundraiser, and if you paid ten bucks, you'd get a certificate that said a planet in some faraway galaxy was named after you. So Mom paid the ten bucks, and I still have the certificate hanging on the wall in my bedroom.

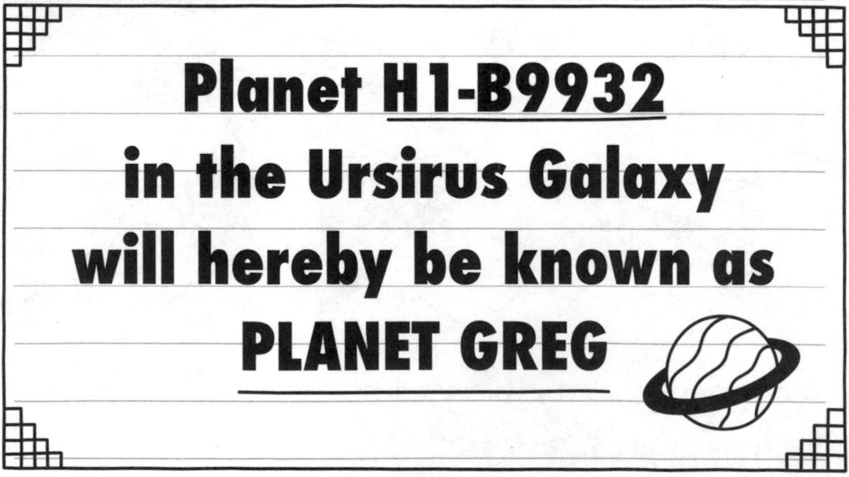

Planet H1-B9932
in the Ursirus Galaxy
will hereby be known as
PLANET GREG

But when Mom filled out the form, I wish she'd put my first AND last name on it. Because now some random Greg could get to my planet before I do and say it's HIS.

Dad said our mistake was that we were going to places everyone knew about, and if we got off the main road, we might find something SPECIAL.

So we took a detour and kept our eyes peeled for anything that looked like it was worth stopping for.

And sure enough, after we took a few more turns, we found a crystal-clear lake with nobody else in SIGHT.

The air-conditioning in Uncle Gary's camper wasn't working, and everyone was ready to cool off. So we got into our bathing suits and took a dip in the lake.

It took a second before I realized something wasn't RIGHT. I noticed a million shimmering objects just beneath the surface, and my mind went right to PIRANHAS. I'm pretty sure everyone ELSE'S did, too.

I was almost to the shore when I felt a bunch of tiny mouths NIBBLING me.

I thought I was being eaten ALIVE. And by the time I made it out of the water, I was surprised to be in one piece.

Or ALMOST in one piece. I had a scab on my knee when I got into the water, but by the time I got out it was totally picked CLEAN.

Just then a truck pulled up, and the two guys inside looked MAD.

That's when we found out the lake we were swimming in was a FISH HATCHERY.

I think those guys were about to call the cops on us for TRESPASSING, and we didn't wanna stick around to find out. So we piled into the camper and Dad stepped on the gas.

The next time Mom makes fish for dinner, I'm definitely gonna check the package to see where they came from first.

The crazy thing is, the fish hatchery wasn't the LAST place we got chased away from today. We tried parking the camper in a meadow so we could get out and enjoy the view while we ate, but it turned out to be somebody's FARM.

We finally found a field that didn't look like it belonged to anyone, so that's where we stopped for the night.

The sleeping situation wasn't great. The kitchen table converted into a BED, which is where Mom and Dad slept.

I wasn't crazy about the idea of eating breakfast off the spot where Dad slept in his boxer shorts.

I had to share the loft above the cabin with Rodrick, which wasn't much of an improvement on our deal in Gramma's basement.

The only person who had any space to himself was Manny. He'd turned one of the cabinets in the kitchenette into a little apartment, and his setup was actually pretty SWEET.

While Mom and Dad were getting ready for bed, I found out a major downside of the camper. The bathroom walls were paper thin, and with the engine off you could hear EVERYTHING happening in there. And trust me, no kid wants to hear his mother's bathroom noises.

Thursday

It turns out the place we stopped for the night was a public park. Little League practice started first thing in the morning, and we were parked right over the pitcher's mound.

Luckily, we were able to take off before some kid broke a taillight with a line drive.

Mom said she didn't want a repeat of yesterday and asked everyone to think of something we could do that was guaranteed FUN. And that's when I remembered a billboard I saw the day before.

The billboard was for this place called the Family Adventure Center. Usually, whenever the word "family" is part of something, it's a warning to stay away. But the pictures on the sign made me think this place could be DIFFERENT.

We had to backtrack about two hours to find the adventure center, but it didn't really matter since we weren't really headed anywhere to begin with.

I have to say, this place was pretty cool. There were a million activities, and I wanted to do them ALL.

But everything had an age and height requirement, and Manny wasn't tall enough to do any GOOD activities.

The only activity Manny was big enough for was the Fun Float, where you drifted down the river in inner tubes. So that's what Mom signed us up for.

I really wanted to do something more exciting, like rock climbing, but Mom was dead set on us all doing something as a family.

Mom said the Fun Float would be RELAXING, and after we put on our life jackets, we grabbed the cooler and a few other things from the camper to take with us on the river.

After our experience with the fish farm yesterday, I wasn't crazy about getting into the water again. But there were a bunch of other people doing the Fun Float, too, and I figured if there were any piranhas in the river, they'd go for THEM before they'd go for ME.

I have to admit that once we got going, it WAS kind of relaxing. Maybe even a little TOO relaxing. Rodrick fell asleep, while Dad answered work emails and Mom checked in with Manny's pediatrician.

So no one was really paying attention when we hit a shallow part in the river and came to a complete STOP. We had to take our tubes out of the water, and it wasn't fun walking across a bunch of sharp rocks in our bare feet.

Once the river got deeper, we put the tubes back in the water. But my inner tube must've got punctured in the shallow part, because it was losing air. So I took Manny's tube, and we emptied the ice out of the cooler so he could use THAT.

I thought the trip was gonna take twenty minutes, but it had already been two HOURS, with no end in sight. And we really slowed down when we got stuck behind a big group of people jamming up the river.

I hit a warm spot in the water, and I've been in enough baby pools to know what THAT meant. So when the river got wider I paddled my tube around those guys to try and get out of their wake.

Unfortunately, I went a little too far and ended up in a part of the river where the water was really ROUGH. And a few seconds later, I got tossed from my inner tube.

It was actually pretty SCARY. The water was moving fast, so I pointed my feet downstream to make sure I didn't crack my head open on a rock.

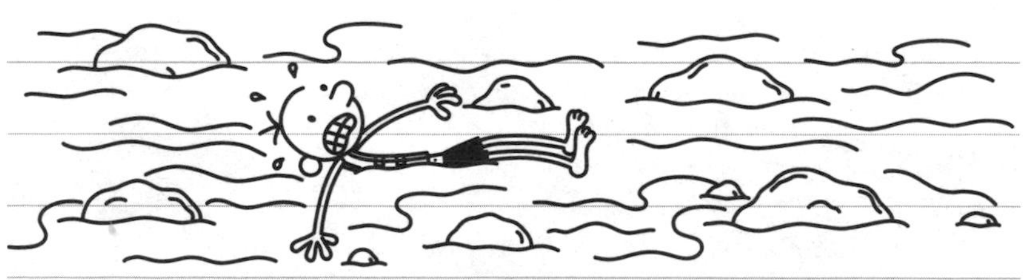

I called out for HELP, but the people around me had their music up too loud to even notice.

My family tried to save me, but it turns out they're totally useless in an emergency.

Up ahead, people were pulling their inner tubes out of the river in the landing area, so I tried to paddle myself over there.

But the water was moving too fast, and I was getting pulled downstream. My family got out of the river, and Dad was yelling and pointing at something near me. That's when I saw a big branch hanging out over the water, and I grabbed it.

For a second, I thought everything was going to be OK. Then I noticed something drifting away from me and realized it was my BATHING SUIT.

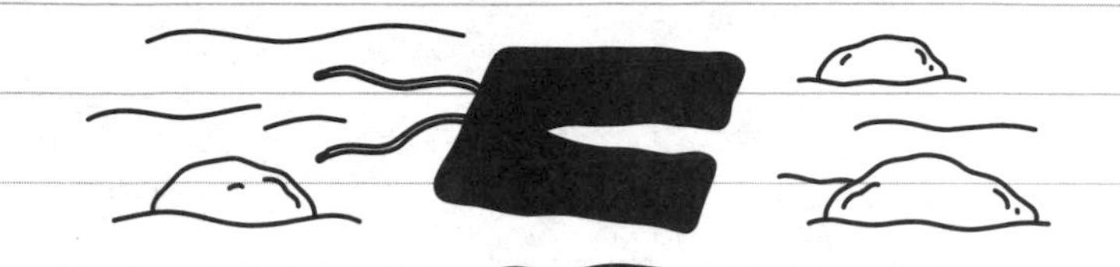

A lifeguard from the adventure center started wading out after me with a life preserver. And I knew if I just kept hanging on to that branch, she'd RESCUE me.

But all I could think of were the people in the landing area who were about to see me without my bathing suit. And Rodrick was already recording me with his phone.

So I decided the best move was to let GO and take my chances.

Luckily, the water wasn't as rocky downstream, but it was still moving fast. By the time I was able to drag myself onto the shore, I must've been a quarter of a mile from the landing area. And I never did find my bathing suit, but thankfully I found the COOLER.

Friday

Last night, everyone in my family agreed that our trip was off to a pretty terrible start. But we couldn't decide what to do NEXT.

I thought we should just admit this trip was a MISTAKE and go back to Gramma's. But Dad said we couldn't turn around now because we hadn't done any actual CAMPING yet.

Dad said there was a national forest a few hours away, and if we camped there, we could stay in one place for the rest of the trip and relax for a change.

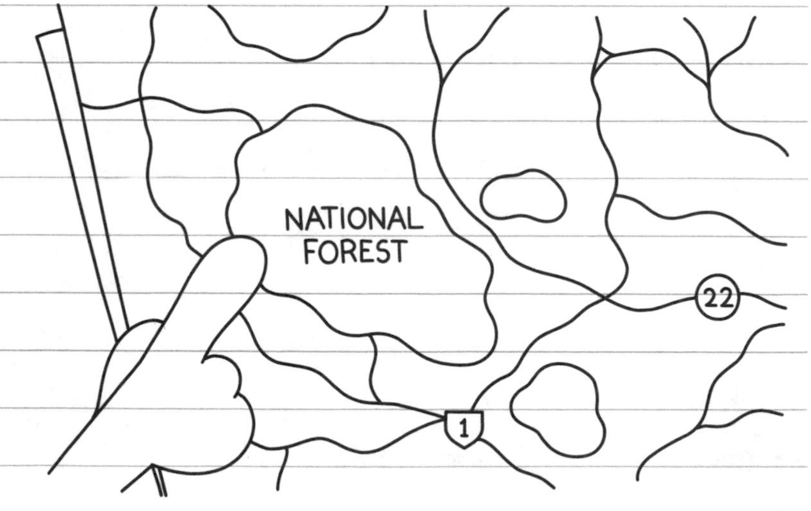

I wasn't crazy about going off on our own, but I knew how the rest of the summer was gonna play out if we went back to Gramma's basement now.

I didn't feel great about camping in the wilderness, but Dad said if we got into any trouble, there were rangers who could help us out. And that made me feel a little better.

So we spent the night in the parking lot of the adventure center, and first thing in the morning we headed for the national forest.

The ranger at the entrance told us it hadn't rained in a few weeks, so the risk of fire was really high. Then she gave Dad a map and a pamphlet with tips on how to camp responsibly.

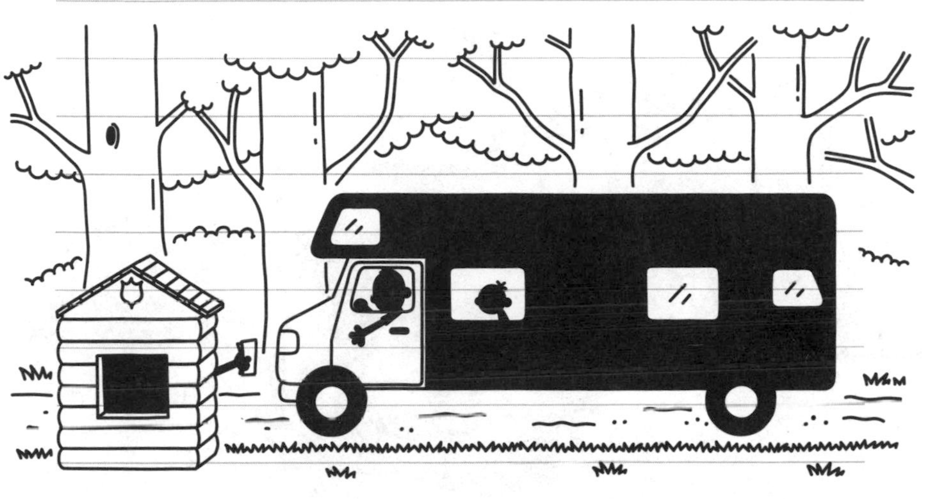

The forest was big, so it took a while for us to get to our campsite. And we didn't see a single human being on our way in.

The campsite was actually really nice. There was a lot of space for the camper, and we were right next to a little stream. After we set up our hammock and chairs, we kicked back and enjoyed being out in nature.

At least MOST of us did. After a few minutes, Mom asked what our "plan" was, and Dad said this WAS the plan.

Mom said we couldn't just sit around all day, and we needed to do something ACTIVE like go on a nature hike or something.

But that sounded like a lot of work to us guys, especially after a long drive. So Mom said if we were all gonna laze around, she was gonna put our electronics in the Vault for the rest of the trip. And that was enough to get us moving.

Mom pulled out the map and found a trail that was nearby. And before we headed off on the hike, she told everyone to fill up our canteens and put on bug spray. But I was a lot more worried about BEARS than bugs.

I remembered that the guy at the camping store said if you saw a bear out in nature, the best thing you could do was make noise to scare it away.

Luckily, Uncle Gary left some pots and pans under the sink in the camper. But I wasn't gonna wait until we SPOTTED a bear to start making a racket.

Everyone got annoyed with me pretty quick, and Mom told me I needed to bring the cookware back to the camper.

She said I could catch up with them farther down the trail, and I was actually fine with that, because that stuff was pretty heavy, anyway. Plus, I was starting to wonder if the noise might actually ATTRACT bears, because whenever I hear pots and pans, I'm thinking DINNER.

After I put the cookware back in the camper, I turned around and got back on the trail. I thought if I hurried it might take me ten minutes to reconnect with everyone. But then I ran into a PROBLEM.

The trail SPLIT, and I didn't know which way my family went.

I figured the odds were 50-50, so I headed LEFT. But I walked for a long time without finding them and figured I must've picked the wrong path. So I went back to the place where the fork in the trail was, and that's where I hit ANOTHER snag.

I was all turned around and couldn't remember which path was the one I hadn't taken yet and which one led back to the camper. And I couldn't tell which was which because to me, every tree and rock looked the SAME.

That's when I started to get WORRIED. I remembered the guy at the camping store saying that sometimes bears will use human trails because it's easier than walking through the brush. So I really didn't feel good about hanging out in the middle of an INTERSECTION.

I've read that a bear's sense of smell is a thousand times better than a human's. So when I pulled out the container of lip balm I had in my pocket, I practically started hyperventilating.

I decided to get off the trail, which turned out to be a dumb move. Because once I was off the path, I couldn't find my way BACK.

My mind started racing, and I thought about what would happen if I was lost for GOOD.

I've read stories about human beings who got cut off from civilization and were raised by WOLVES. I didn't know if there were any wolves in this forest, but there were plenty of SQUIRRELS.

Luckily, my family found me before things could get too crazy. Because in another hour or two I might've been too far gone.

When we got back to camp, Mom asked Rodrick to check me for ticks, since I'd been off the trail. He looked me over and told me I had a HUGE tick right in the middle of my back.

Rodrick said the tick must've been on me for a while, because it looked like it was about to BURST. And I almost passed out when he showed me the picture he took on his phone.

It turns out it was just a JOKE, and the picture was something Rodrick found online. But even after I KNEW it was a joke, I still felt like something was in the middle of my back for the rest of the day.

Mom said everyone should take a shower, since it had been two days and we were starting to stink. Rodrick went first, and he was in there for at least half an hour. So when it was my turn, there was no hot water left.

Dad checked the propane tank and said it was empty, which meant it was cold showers from now on. No one was happy about that, especially MOM.

I noticed it was really starting to SMELL in the bathroom, so I told Dad. He said the reason it stunk was because we hadn't emptied out the sewage tank yet.

To be honest with you, I didn't even THINK about what happened to our waste in the camper.

Back home, when you flush the toilet, everything gets magically whisked away to some faraway place. But in a camper, you're actually carrying that stuff around WITH you.

If I had known that beforehand, I'm not sure I would've agreed to go on this trip.

Now I was starting to worry about what happened if the tank OVERFLOWED. So today, whenever someone looked like they needed to go number two, I'd try to talk them into taking it somewhere ELSE.

I guess I should be grateful we live in a time when toilets even EXIST. Rodrick told me that the guy who invented the flushing toilet was named Thomas Crapper. And I don't know if that's true or if it's another one of his jokes.

If it's TRUE, I hope that guy made a ton of money. Because I wouldn't want a body function named after ME.

Dad got a fire going and cooked some beef stew. He was gonna serve baked beans to go with it, but Rodrick left the can too close to the fire, and that was the end of THAT.

After dinner, we tied up our trash and hoisted it in a tree with a rope, like the guy at the camping store told us to. I figured if any bear was smart enough to get at our trash, then they deserved to have it.

By now it was dark out, and Mom said we should turn in for the night. But Dad said the best part of camping was sitting around the campfire under the stars.

That got Mom all EXCITED and she tried to get us to join in on a song that she said she learned at summer camp when she was a kid. But the rest of us aren't real big on sing-alongs, so we just waited for Mom to wrap it up.

After that, Dad brought out some marshmallows, and we found some long sticks.

While we were roasting our marshmallows over the fire, Dad got all serious. He told us that a long time ago he went camping with his dad, and they'd met a crusty old ranger who told them a crazy story.

The ranger said he used to have a beagle named Matilda, and she'd follow him wherever he'd go. But then this one night the ranger made a FIRE, and he saw a weird creature with glowing red eyes prowling around the edge of the camp.

Matilda chased after the creature, and the ranger tracked her deep into the woods. But the only trace of the dog was her broken collar lying on the ground.

Dad said that every night, the ranger would sleep in his cabin alone, hoping Matilda would find her way back to him. And on nights just like tonight, when there was a crescent moon, he'd hear the howl of a beagle deep in the woods.

Mom wasn't happy with Dad for telling that story because Manny seemed really shook up. And to be honest, I was a little spooked, too.

Then I heard a sound coming from deep in the woods that made my heart STOP.

For a split second I thought it was the ghost of Matilda. But then I realized Rodrick was missing, and the whole thing was one big joke Dad and Rodrick were playing on the rest of us.

But it kind of BACKFIRED. Because when Rodrick howled, Manny JUMPED. And that's how Dad ended up with a flaming marshmallow stuck to his knee.

I think Dad was about to dive in the stream to put out the fire, but luckily Rodrick remembered where we kept the fire extinguisher.

Mom started giving Dad a lecture about why you should never scare people, but she got cut off by weird noises coming from the forest. At first I thought it might be another JOKE, but the look in Dad's and Rodrick's eyes told me it WASN'T.

Whatever was out there sounded BIG and was coming our way. So we piled into the camper and locked the door behind us.

Sure enough, it was a BEAR. But it wasn't after our trash, it was after the BAKED BEANS.

Once the bear was done licking the beans off the camper, it wanted MORE. And I wish I could say we stayed calm, but I'd be lying.

Dad climbed into the driver's seat to get us OUT of there, but the keys were by the fire. And when the bear started rocking the camper, I thought it was OVER for us.

I guess Manny did, too, because he managed to scramble out of a window and get up on the ROOF. And he brought the flare gun WITH him.

Saturday

Last night, the light from the flare scared off the bear, so when the ranger arrived at our campsite, we didn't really need to be RESCUED anymore. By then, our biggest problem was the marshmallow burn on Dad's knee.

The ranger said it was totally reckless for us to shoot off that flare, because it could've started a forest fire. Then she said we were gonna have to leave the park first thing in the morning.

Well, that was fine with ME. We lasted one night in the wilderness, and I didn't think we could survive ANOTHER.

When we left the park this morning, I was really looking forward to getting back to Gramma's basement. I knew we'd have plenty of hot water and no BEARS.

But Mom wasn't ready to go back home just yet. She said the reason we had a bad time camping was because we were too ISOLATED, and if we went to a place where there were other PEOPLE, we'd have more fun.

Mom told us she'd heard of these RV parks where they have all sorts of activities for families, and everything you need is in one place.

Then she started looking up nearby RV parks and found one that had potential.

What caught my eye was the word "luxury." After getting a taste of "real" camping, I was ready for something a little more UPSCALE.

I knew from Sunday school that "Eden" was another word for paradise, so that sounded promising.

The way I remember it, Adam and Eve got kicked out of the Garden of Eden because one of them was tempted to eat an apple from a forbidden tree.

If it was ME, I wouldn't have given up paradise for a piece of fruit. It would've had to have been for something GOOD, like a TWINKIE.

It took us most of the day to get to Campers' Eden. But when we crossed over the bridge and got our first look at the place, I could see why they named it the way they did.

We pulled up to the lodge and went inside, where a staffer told us about all the awesome stuff they had at the campground, like a game room and a pool and horseshoe pits, plus a lake with canoes and kayaks.

There was also a bathhouse where you could take a hot shower, which was the thing MOM was most excited about.

What I liked was that each campsite had its own sewer hookup. The inside of our camper was starting to smell like a monkey house, and I was really looking forward to our sewage tank getting flushed out.

Mom told the staffer we'd like a campsite with a lake view. But the woman told Mom that people booked those WAY ahead of time, and that the only spots left were in the economy lot.

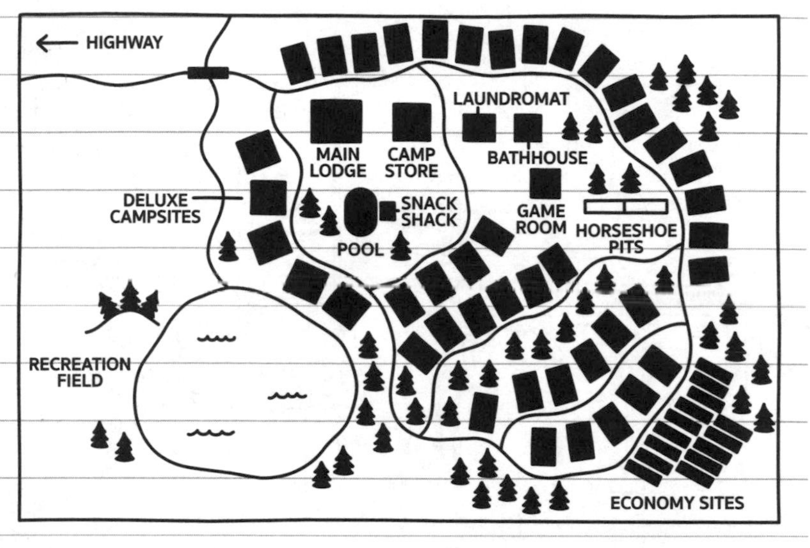

I guess Mom was focused on that hot shower, so she said we'd take whatever they HAD. And after we paid up for the week, we drove our camper down the hill to find our site.

The farther down the hill we went, the smaller the campsites got. And when we found our spot, Dad could barely fit the camper onto the concrete pad.

After we parked, Mom unloaded the camping chairs while Dad tried to figure out how to flush the sewage tank. I wanted to be as far away as possible when he got THAT process started, so I told Mom and Dad I was gonna go off and explore the campground.

I wanted to check out the game room, so that's where I went first. There were a few arcade machines in there, but nothing I was really interested in playing.

They had a pool table, but from what I could tell it didn't have any actual BALLS.

I checked out the swimming pool next, and that was kind of a disappointment, too. It was full of little kids, and their parents weren't even keeping an eye on them.

Nowadays, kids wear these floaty vests, so they don't even have to learn how to swim. It's not like when I was growing up, when you had to learn the HARD way.

Some of the little kids drifted out into the deep end, which was a problem because people were doing cannonballs off the high dive.

There was no lifeguard on duty, so everyone was pretty much doing whatever they WANTED.

I didn't really feel safe going in the pool, so I decided to relax in the hot tub instead. But that's when I found out that this place wasn't joking around about the "pet-friendly" thing.

There was a snack shack in the pool area, and the laundromat and bathhouse were close by.

I wanted to kill a little more time before I went back to our camper in case Dad wasn't done emptying out the sewage tank. So I explored some of the other campsites to see what they were like.

The nicest ones were the deluxe campsites that overlooked the stream. Those people had satellite dishes and fancy grills, and they had actual LAWNS that they took care of.

I could tell the deluxe campsite people didn't like us economy guys hanging around their properties, though, so I didn't stick around long.

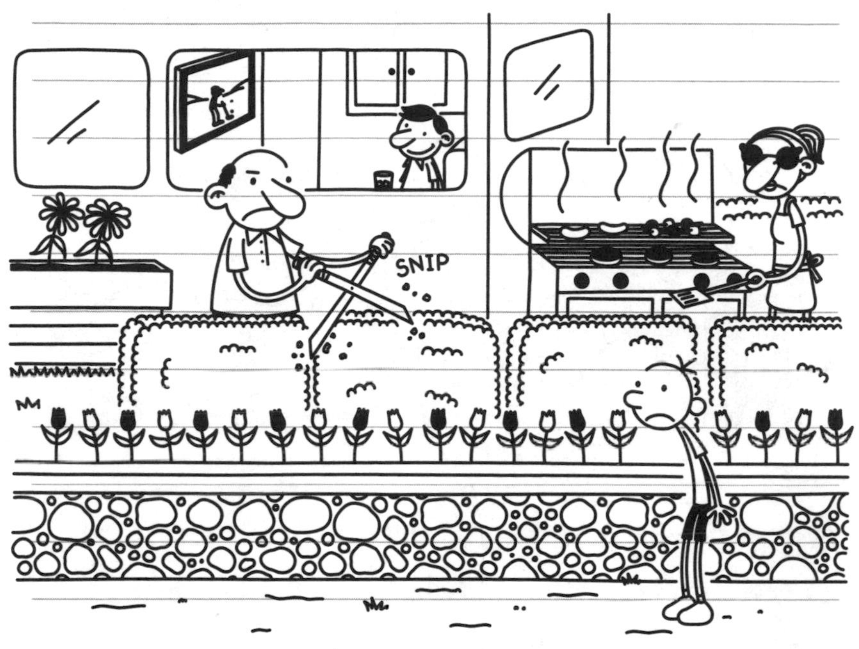

The spots farther down the hill weren't as nice, but each row was kind of like its own little neighborhood.

One of the rows had a bunch of older people in it, so I'm guessing that was the area for retirees. A few rows down were families with little kids.

Some of the rows had THEMES, and people went kind of crazy with the decorations.

A few people didn't have full-sized campers, and I felt grateful that Uncle Gary hadn't left us one of THOSE instead.

Some other people didn't have campers at ALL. There was one campsite that looked like it had a full motorcycle gang in it, and I was glad we didn't end up as neighbors with THOSE guys.

But it might've been even WORSE if we ended up in the pet-friendly row. Because that area was a total ZOO.

I could tell when I was getting closer to the economy row because the campsites were packed a whole lot TIGHTER, and people had to make the most of their space.

When I got back to our campsite, Dad was cooking hot dogs on the grill. I wanted to ask him if he washed his hands after doing the sewage hookup, but I thought he might get annoyed with me.

Mom was trying to get to know some of our neighbors, but they seemed like the type of people who liked to keep to themselves.

Once Dad was done cooking, we sat down at our picnic table to eat. But the people on the other side of us were playing cornhole on their roof, and somebody up there had lousy aim.

While we were cleaning up the mess, I told Mom and Dad I thought coming here might've been a MISTAKE. But Mom said sometimes it's hard getting used to a new place, and I just needed to give it a chance.

Then she reminded me that we hadn't even visited the lake yet, which should be the best part. I was about to say something else, when I got interrupted by a noise coming from the direction of the main lodge.

It sounded like one of those air-raid sirens you hear in a war movie when enemy bombers are approaching, and it put me totally on edge.

Our next-door neighbors seemed nervous, too, and they gathered up their stuff to take inside their camper.

When Dad asked what the siren was for, our neighbor said it meant there was a SKUNK on the property, and everyone needed to get inside in a hurry.

Well, that was enough to get US moving. We shut our door and peeked out of the window while we waited. Sure enough, a few minutes later, a skunk came sniffing around our campsite.

It got up on the picnic table, and when it started eating our hot dogs, there was nothing we could do but WATCH.

Once the skunk was done eating, it LEFT. After a while, the siren stopped and everyone came back outside. And even though the skunk was GONE, the whole campsite smelled TERRIBLE.

Dad said the reason it smelled so bad was because there's some sort of chemical in a skunk's glands that people can smell from a mile away. And he said if you got SPRAYED by a skunk, it would be a thousand times WORSE.

He said the best thing you could do if you ran into a skunk was to back away slowly, because a skunk will only spray a person if it feels like it's cornered or threatened.

Then he said you know you're about to be sprayed if a skunk stands on its front legs and wiggles its butt. But by then it's probably too LATE.

Rodrick said that a skunk's spray doesn't just smell bad, it's FLAMMABLE, too. I don't know if that's true or if it's just another one of his lies. If it IS true, then once skunks figure out how to light matches, us human beings are in BIG trouble.

When God created the animals, he gave them all cool stuff to defend themselves with, like shells and talons and claws.

But then when the time came to create PEOPLE, all the GOOD ideas were used up.

I guess God made up for it by giving us big BRAINS. But if it was up to me, I probably would've gone with QUILLS.

I figure if something as small as a skunk could scare off predators by smelling bad, then maybe it could work for ME. And that's when I decided I'm not gonna shower until I finish high school.

I probably shouldn't have told MOM my plan, though, because all it did was remind her that I skipped taking a shower today. So now she's making me take one first thing tomorrow morning.

Luckily, we had a few extra hot dogs in the camper, and Dad cooked them over the fire. But I kept thinking about that skunk. So I was already a little jumpy when all of a sudden we got SPRAYED.

But it wasn't a SKUNK that sprayed us. It was one of our NEIGHBORS. Apparently, 9:00 is "lights out" at camp, and I guess people around here take that pretty seriously.

So we turned in for the night, but I didn't really SLEEP. Because like I said before, those economy campsites were packed together TIGHT.

Sunday

It turned out the whole camp was early to bed, early to rise. We didn't even need to set our alarm clocks because our neighbors let us know when it was time to get up.

Believe it or not, some guy was doing WOOD CARVINGS at his campsite. I wanted to give him a piece of my mind, but when I saw the chain saw, I figured maybe I could let it slide this one time.

After Dad got out of bed, he started cooking pancakes and eggs on the griddle. Mom was just getting back from the bathhouse and she gave me the scoop on how things worked up there.

She said you had to pay for the shower with quarters, and gave me a few. Then she told me that I needed to stop by the laundromat and move our clothes from the washer to the dryer.

I really didn't like the idea of taking a shower in a public building. When you live in a house with your family, the bathroom is the only place you can get any PRIVACY. So when I'm in there, I'm in my own little world.

And once that door's locked, I can do anything I WANT.

But sometimes I get myself in TROUBLE in the bathroom. Once, I almost broke my ribs when I was pretending to be Spider-Man in the shower.

When I arrived at the bathhouse, the line was already wrapped around the building. And I got to know my fellow campers a little better than I WANTED to.

I figured the line would split at the entrance, and guys would go one way and girls would go the other. But it turns out this place didn't have those kinds of boundaries.

I found out the reason the wait was so long was because there were only three shower stalls inside. When it was finally my turn, I put a quarter in the coin slot on the stall door, and that got the shower going.

The hot water felt GOOD, especially since I hadn't had a hot shower in a few days.

But I couldn't really enjoy it since the stalls only went so high.

I closed my eyes and tried to pretend I was by myself. But that was kind of hard to do when the person in the next stall started getting CHATTY.

I decided to wrap things up and get out of there. But the shower stopped before I had a chance to rinse the shampoo out of my hair.

It turns out one quarter only paid for three minutes of hot water. I tried to hand the next person in line a quarter to put in the slot, but I couldn't get his attention.

So I stepped out of the shower to put the coin in MYSELF. But I guess that was just the opportunity this guy was WAITING for.

And what REALLY stunk was when he started using my SHAMPOO.

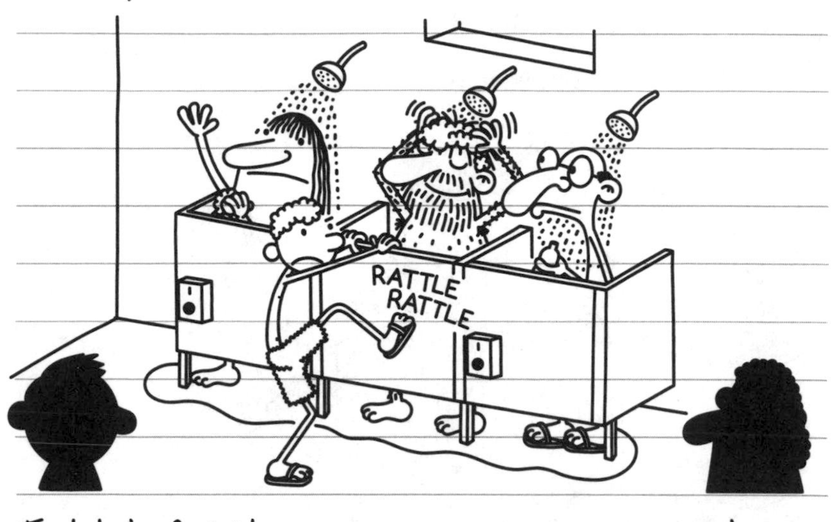

I didn't feel like getting in an argument with a naked guy, so I LEFT. But some soapsuds got in my eye, and I could barely see where I was going.

Luckily, I found my way to the laundromat, where there was a sink. And that water was FREE.

Once I finished rinsing the shampoo out of my hair, I started looking for our clothes. But someone had taken them out of the washing machine and dumped them on the floor so they could put THEIR clothes in.

After I put our clothes in the dryer, I decided I was gonna stick around the washing machines and find out who dumped our stuff on the floor when they came back to get THEIRS.

But when I saw who it WAS, I thought maybe I could let things slide one more time.

When I got back to our campsite, all I wanted to do was crawl back into bed. But Mom said we were all going down to the lake and I needed to put on my bathing suit.

I reminded her that I didn't HAVE a bathing suit anymore, and I was hoping that would get me off the hook. But Mom said Rodrick had a SPARE, and even though I'm not a fan of wearing someone else's clothes, I knew there was no point in debating her about it.

I figured if we splashed around the lake for a few minutes and acted like we were having a good time, Mom would be satisfied and let us go back to camp. But she brought her camera with her, and that always complicates things.

This summer, Mom's been spending a lot of time on social media. And whenever she sees how perfect her friends' families look, it makes her JEALOUS.

So Mom always puts us in these awkward poses to make it look like WE'RE having a good time, too. But there must be something wrong with my family, because we can never get our act together.

The lake looked calm and peaceful when we first saw it from the bridge. But today, it was a whole different scene.

I was expecting the lake to be clear, like the one at the fish hatchery, but it looked DIRTY to me. And that's probably because people weren't just using it for SWIMMING.

I thought people were acting kind of nuts at the POOL yesterday, but at the lake it was at a whole different LEVEL.

There was a rope swing attached to a big tree that went out over the water. But I wasn't planning on using that thing unless it RAINED for a few days first.

There were some rafts floating in the middle of the lake, and I thought about grabbing one. But I changed my mind when I saw how people were using them.

There was a ramp at the bottom of a big hill by the lake, and I couldn't tell what it was for. But my question got answered when some kid launched himself into the water inside a tractor tire.

Mom wanted us all to swim, but I was still pretty scarred from my LAST experience in a lake. Plus, I don't trust any water I can't see through.

There was something weird sticking up in the middle of the lake, and I pointed it out to Dad. He said it was probably just a branch, but it didn't look like a branch to ME. And when you can only see a part of something, it could be ANYTHING.

Nobody else was in the mood to swim, either, so we put our stuff down on the ground. But it turned out a lake shore isn't the same as a BEACH shore, and within a few seconds we were sinking in the muck.

Mom said we weren't going back to our campsite until we did something FUN. There was a canoe tied up to the dock, and she said we should take it out on the water. I was fine with being on top of the water, so long as we didn't have to go IN it.

We took turns getting into the canoe, which wasn't as easy as I thought it would be.

I stayed low, just like Dad told me to. Rodrick DIDN'T, though, and we almost capsized while we were still tied to the dock.

After we were all in the canoe, we put on life jackets and paddled out on the water. But some people swimming nearby seemed like they were in a hurry to get out of our WAY.

Then we found out WHY. As soon as we got to the middle of the lake, something BIG landed right next to our canoe. And a second later, there was ANOTHER splash.

Some teenagers up on the hill had turned a hammock into a giant SLINGSHOT, and they were using us for TARGET practice.

I guess that explained why no one was using the canoe. We tried to paddle back to the dock, but the guys on the hill were getting more and more accurate with each shot.

I guess Rodrick didn't wanna get hit, so he decided to abandon ship. And that was a problem for the REST of us, because now we were unbalanced.

Our canoe capsized, and somehow me and Dad ended up UNDERNEATH it. At first I thought it was a GOOD thing, since we were protected from those watermelons.

But I changed my mind when we took a direct hit, because it was like being on the inside of a DRUM.

Me and Dad ditched the canoe and swam for the dock. And we had to move FAST, because now we were out of range, so the guys on the hill were SKIPPING their shots.

We pulled ourselves onto the dock, where we were safe. Mom was upset because her camera was ruined, but I didn't really want my picture taken right at that moment, anyway.

Monday

I think Mom realized we'd had a little too much family time yesterday, because this morning she said everyone could go do their own thing. I was planning on relaxing for once, but Mom had OTHER ideas.

She said this camp was full of kids my age, and this was the perfect opportunity to branch out and make new FRIENDS.

I told Mom I wasn't really in the mood for socializing, and there wasn't any point in trying to make new friends since I'd never even SEE any of these people again.

But Mom said some of her best friends to this day are people she met at summer camp when she was MY age.

I told Mom it's DIFFERENT from when she was growing up, and it's a lot harder to make friends with strangers nowadays. But Mom said she could help me with that.

I was hoping Mom would just drop it. But ten minutes later, a group of boys passed by our camper carrying fishing poles. And before I could STOP her, Mom started in with the introductions.

Luckily, these kids didn't beat me up the second Mom stepped away. They said they were going down to their fishing spot, and I could come with them if I wanted.

I'm not really big on fishing, but I figured I'd just go along with these guys to make Mom happy.

I recognized a few of them from the pool, and on our way down to the stream I learned their names.

Everyone was calling the smallest kid Juicebox, and he seemed to be the one in charge. The kid with the inner tube was Big Marcus, and I couldn't tell if he was wearing that thing for fun or if he couldn't actually get OUT of it.

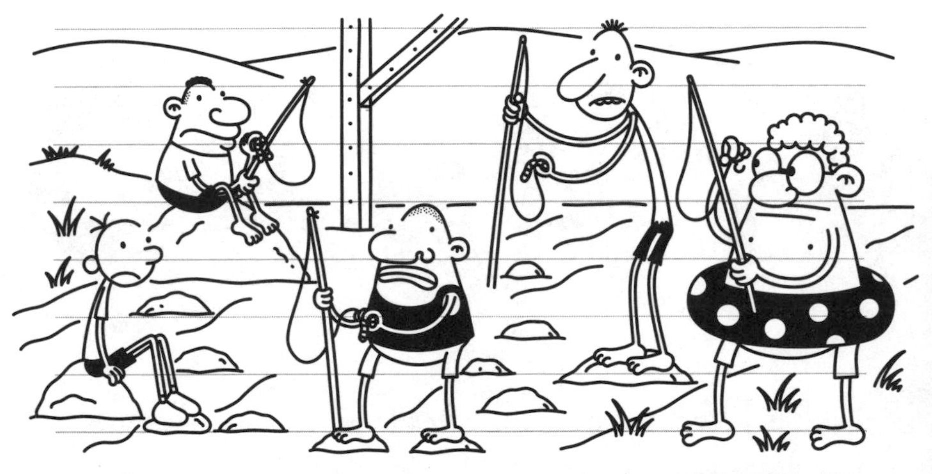

The tall skinny kid was Weevil, and the boy with the shaved head was called DooDoo. I don't wanna be mean or anything, but that boy really lived up to his nickname.

A few other kids joined us, and THEY all had nicknames, too. So I guess that's a thing around here.

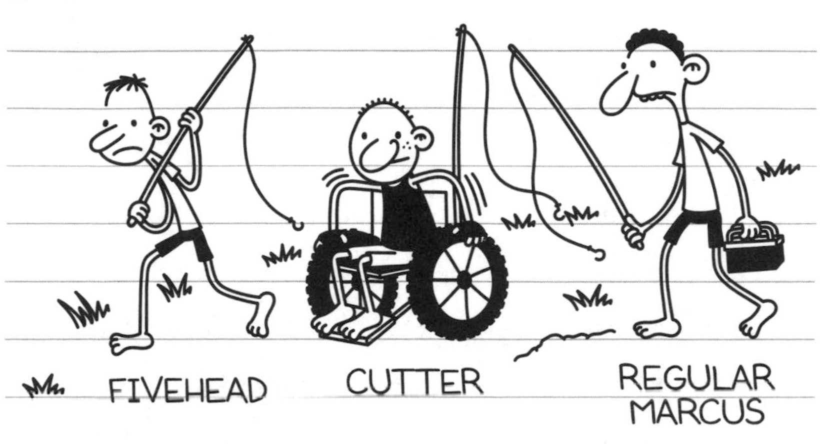

Juicebox asked me MY name, and I figured since everyone ELSE was using made-up names, I might as well, too.

The stream was pretty shallow in this spot, so I didn't see how these guys were gonna catch any fish. But I found out the real reason they came here wasn't to fish, it was to TALK. And they argued about EVERYTHING.

The first topic was which superhero would win in a fight, and that turned into a conversation about which superpower was best. And somehow that turned into a debate about what kind of animal you'd choose to fight if you were sentenced to death.

Then they got in an argument about whether it would be better to fight a person with the head of a shark or a shark with the head of a person. And the guys were split down the middle on that one.

The conversation got pretty heated, and then it got PHYSICAL. I didn't wanna get hurt, so I tried to stay out of the way.

But just like that it was OVER, and everyone acted like nothing happened.

I was starting to get nervous hanging around a bunch of guys who liked to settle things with their FISTS, and I told them maybe I should be heading back. But Juicebox said that since I was the NEW kid around here, it was their job to show me the ropes. And I decided to go along with it, mostly because I didn't want DooDoo putting me in a headlock.

It turns out these guys have been coming here for years, so they knew all the ins and outs of the place. They knew how to get a free bag of pretzels from the vending machine at the lodge, the exact time the delivery truck came to resupply the camp store, and where you needed to be when they threw out the day-old donuts.

Plus, they knew where all the cute girls in camp were staying and when they each ate lunch.

These guys were big pranksters, too. Weevil found a half-filled bottle of shampoo on the ground, and that gave Juicebox an IDEA. He took us around the back of the bathhouse to the wall on the other side of the shower stalls.

As soon as the person near the window finished rinsing the soapsuds out of his hair, Juicebox squirted more shampoo on his scalp.

The guy lathered up his hair AGAIN, and once he finished rinsing it, Juicebox was there with another squirt. After a couple more rounds of this, the guy started going CRAZY.

But when he heard Cutter laugh, we were BUSTED. And it was the LAST guy we should've been messing with, too.

Luckily, Juicebox and his gang knew all the good hiding spots on the campground, so we laid low behind the snack shack until the coast was clear.

I'd never really had a group of friends before, and I was starting to have FUN.

The guys wanted to go down to the field by the lake and play some games. I figured they wanted to play something normal like kickball or freeze tag, so I went along with them.

But these guys had their OWN idea of fun.

And most of their games involved someone getting hit by a ball or getting tackled, and sometimes both at the same time.

The last game we played was Red Rover, where everyone makes a human chain and tries to keep one person from getting through. But Big Marcus was unstoppable, and we got pretty banged up.

It seemed like everyone was ready to wrap things up for the day, but that's when something fell from the SKY.

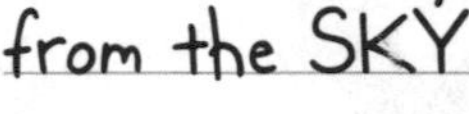

It was those teenagers on the hill, launching watermelons from their hammock. We ran for cover underneath the shed where they kept the kayaks. And that's where Juicebox told me what was going on.

He said that every time him and his gang played in that field, the teenagers bombarded them with watermelons. And I really wished someone had mentioned that to me BEFORE I agreed to come down there.

But Juicebox said that today, him and his guys were ready to strike BACK.

They'd stashed a bunch of water guns in one of the kayaks, and they had some serious firepower in there. Everyone chose a weapon for themselves, but since I was the new guy, I picked LAST.

I wasn't crazy about picking a fight with a bunch of teenagers anyway, so I told the guys I really needed to be getting back to my family.

But Juicebox said I was one of THEM now, and we were all in this fight TOGETHER. I probably should've walked away then, but I didn't wanna let these guys down.

We gathered around Juicebox, and he showed us his plan. He said somebody needed to volunteer to be the decoy on the lake so the rest of us could sneak up on the teenagers from behind.

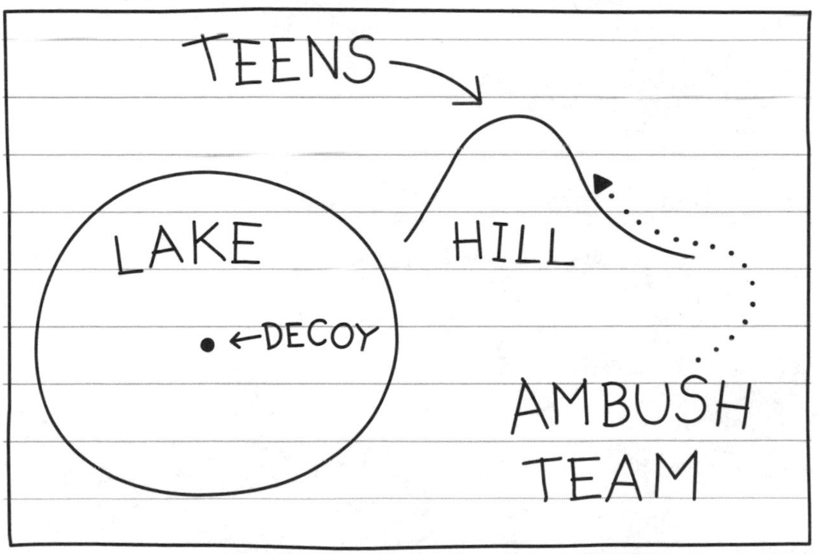

Nobody wanted to volunteer, so we took a vote, and that's how Big Marcus got chosen. And that was good news for me, because I got his water gun.

Big Marcus paddled out to the middle of the lake, and sure enough, the teenagers opened fire as soon as they saw him.

And that's when the rest of us made our MOVE.

SPLORGE

We let loose with everything we had, and by the time our water guns were empty, those teenagers were totally DRENCHED.

But I wish Juicebox had put a little more thought into the NEXT step of his plan, because all we really did was make those guys MAD.

They chased us past the main lodge, and we turned the corner at the laundromat. I thought they were gonna catch us for sure, but Big Marcus picked the PERFECT time to rejoin the team.

That bought the rest of us extra TIME, and we used it to reload our water guns from the soda dispenser at the snack shack.

Cutter grabbed a few squeeze bottles of ketchup and mustard for some extra firepower. So when the teenagers arrived, we were READY for them.

And I don't know if it was the soda or the ketchup that did it, but a few seconds later the snack shack was full of BEES.

We ran to the hiding spot we used earlier in the day and took a minute to catch our breath.

Everyone was in the mood to celebrate, but Juicebox seemed WORRIED. He said those teenagers would be coming for us, and that the camp director was gonna be mad we made a mess at the snack shack.

Cutter said we should make a PACT that if one of us got caught, nobody would rat anyone else out. And everyone seemed to like that idea.

But it got complicated when we started talking about what the penalty was for BREAKING the pact, because everyone had a different idea of what that should be.

Big Marcus said that if you broke the pact, then you had to go through the Pool Noodle Gauntlet, which sounded pretty HARSH to me.

Regular Marcus said that if one of us snitched, that person needed to wear his underwear on his head for a whole day.

Some people wanted to take it even FURTHER. Fivehead said it had to be your DAD'S underwear, and you had to walk past the pretty girls' campsites at lunchtime.

Then the guys got into an argument about whether the underwear should be clean or dirty, and things got physical again. But I was actually GLAD, because it gave me the opportunity I needed to slip away.

Tuesday

Thankfully, Mom didn't have any big plans for us today. Because after everything that happened yesterday, I really just wanted to lie low for the rest of the trip.

Mom went to the camp store to pick up some groceries for dinner, and when she came back, she was all excited about a flyer she'd picked up at the main lodge.

Nobody else was crazy about going to a pool party, but Mom said this could be just the thing to turn our trip around.

We all knew that once Mom gets an idea in her head, there's no talking her out of it. Plus, it had been really sticky and hot all day, so I figured it would be nice to cool off for a few hours.

Mom forgot to get plastic utensils at the store, so she sent me up there with some money. I was a little nervous one of those teenagers might spot me on the way, so I wanted to get there and back as quick as I could.

But I stopped when Regular Marcus called out to me when I passed by the place we hid yesterday.

Regular Marcus told me that this morning, these posters started appearing all over camp, and he showed me one he took from the laundromat.

The second I saw the poster, I knew it was a TRICK. I told Regular Marcus that the people who run this place were just trying to catch the kids who trashed the snack shack, and they were using ice cream as BAIT. I told him not to fall for it, and to tell the OTHER guys not to, either.

But he said it was already too LATE. Because when the first posters went up, Juicebox and the other guys had headed straight for the lodge with their water guns.

Regular Marcus said he would've been WITH them, but he had to go back to his camper to grab his squirt gun. And by the time he got to the lodge, the doors were already LOCKED.

So Regular Marcus climbed up on a recycling bin to look through the window and see what was going on. And what he saw wasn't PRETTY.

It turns out there was no ice cream at ALL. The camp director told the guys they were gonna have to scrub every inch of the snack shack tomorrow morning, and use TOOTHBRUSHES to do it.

I guess Juicebox didn't like the sound of that, so he told the camp director the whole thing was a big MISUNDERSTANDING.

He said him and the other guys got roped into the fight, and the guy that started it all was still on the loose. And when the camp director asked him the name of the "ringleader," Juicebox threw the new guy under the bus.

But I guess the camp director wasn't convinced. Because after he let the other guys go, he made Juicebox walk door to door with him to find this Jimmy Dogfish character.

I really didn't wanna be there when they reached MY camper. So when I got back to our campsite, I told everyone we needed to eat quick so we could get to that pool party.

I figured the pool might be the one place on the campground where I was actually SAFE. But once we got there, I realized I was wrong about that.

It seemed like the combination of loud music and nighttime was making people a little extra crazy. And it wasn't just the kids this time, it was the grown-ups, too.

A bunch of dads had turned the shallow end into a giant WHIRLPOOL.

And somebody had greased the slide, so people were coming off that thing at a hundred miles an hour.

There was a movie playing on a screen at the deep end of the pool, and whoever chose the film probably should've picked something that was a little more family-friendly.

Mom wasn't even paying attention to what was going on in the pool. There were a bunch of activities in the grassy area, and she wanted us to participate in EVERYTHING.

We entered the balloon-popping relay as a family, but we came in last place since Manny didn't have enough body weight to burst the first balloon.

Mom made Dad enter the beer belly contest, but he didn't even make it past the first round.

Manny entered a hot dog eating contest on his own, and I had no IDEA that boy could pack so much food away.

Me and Rodrick competed in a dizzy stick relay race, where you had to spin around a baseball bat five times, then tag the next person on your team. But we were playing against two guys who had just finished the hot dog eating contest, so things got a little MESSY.

Mom tried to get me to enter a mother-son dance contest with her, but there wasn't enough money in the world to get me to agree to THAT.

I entered the pie eating contest, because I thought I might actually WIN. But they held it at the same time as the belly flop contest, and my seat was the one closest to the pool.

Speaking of the belly flop contest, too many contestants got on the diving board at the same time, and it wasn't built to carry that much weight.

After the party activities wrapped up, Mom talked us all into getting in the water for a quick family swim.

The pool was crowded and nobody was really doing any swimming, anyway. It seemed like the only people having any fun were the ones on RAFTS.

But the rafts were all taken, and it didn't look like anybody was willing to give one up.

Then Mom spotted a giant empty inner tube in the middle of the pool. That thing was so big it must've been an AIRPLANE tire or something. So we all swam out to it before someone else took it for themselves.

The tire was so huge it was almost impossible to get into. But with a little teamwork, we finally did it.

Once we all got on, we found out why that thing was empty to BEGIN with.

After we got tossed from the giant inner tube, Mom was done with the pool party. And I felt bad because I knew how much she wanted tonight to be special.

A lot of other people were starting to clear out, too, but there were still a few stragglers coming into the party. And some of them looked FAMILIAR.

The rest of my family got out of the pool, but I decided to stay put. I didn't know if those teenagers would recognize me or not, but I wasn't willing to take any CHANCES.

There were still a lot of people in the pool, so it wasn't that hard to stay hidden. But when those guys stepped in the water, it got harder for me to stay out of sight.

And my situation got a whole lot WORSE when the next two people showed up at the party.

I knew the camp director was looking for ME. So I decided to go in the only direction I could, which was DOWN.

I went to the bottom of the pool and sat there. And I planned on STAYING down there as long as it took.

I was actually starting to run out of oxygen when something WEIRD happened. There was a flash of light, like someone took a picture underwater. And then everyone started getting out of the pool.

Ten seconds later, it was empty except for ME. And that's when I came to the surface.

The first thing I noticed was the RAIN, which was really coming down. Then LIGHTNING flashed across the sky, and that explained why everyone was in such a hurry to get out of the pool.

The teenagers and Juicebox were long gone, and so was my FAMILY. I really didn't wanna get electrocuted, so I figured I'd better get out of there, too.

I left the pool area and headed for the camper. But in the dark and the rain, it was hard to see where I was going.

There was a HUGE crash of lightning, and it sounded like it might've hit something nearby.

Then the air-raid siren on top of the lodge cranked up, which made everything even more STRESSFUL.

I realized that if I stayed outside much longer, I was gonna get burnt to a CRISP. But nobody in any of the deluxe campers would let me inside.

I finally made it to our camper. And when I opened the door, my whole family was already there.

Mom said she thought I'd run ahead to the camper when the rain started, and it was a MIRACLE I was OK.

To be honest with you, I felt the same way.

That storm came at the perfect moment, and I almost felt like it was the work of a higher power.

Or maybe it was just one big cosmic JOKE.

Because if there's one thing I learned tonight, it's that God has a sense of HUMOR.

Wednesday

If you've ever wondered what it's like to be sprayed by a skunk, I can tell you from firsthand experience. It feels like you've gone BLIND, and your eyes sting like CRAZY.

So you have to flush them out with water, if you're lucky enough to have any nearby.

Once your vision improves, you start to notice the SMELL, which is like a mix of rotten eggs and roadkill. And you don't just SMELL it, you TASTE it. But trust me, the best thing is to not get sprayed in the FIRST place.

One of the books we bought at the camping store had a chapter on what you should do if you got sprayed by a skunk. But it wasn't that helpful, since we couldn't get any of the ingredients until the store opened in the morning.

SO YOU'VE BEEN SKUNKED

Getting sprayed by a skunk is no laughing matter. But if it happens to you, here's what you can do to remove the smell:

- Fill a bathtub with 10 pints of 3 percent hydrogen peroxide, 20 tablespoons baking soda, and 10 teaspoons liquid dish soap.
- Bathe, rinse, lather, and repeat as necessary!

We knew we couldn't go to sleep smelling like skunk, so we tried to find something to cover up the odor.

Luckily, there were a bunch of ketchup and mustard packets in one of the drawers, and we rubbed the condiments all over ourselves. Manny found a bottle of Uncle Gary's cologne between the seat cushions, but that stuff smelled almost as bad as the SKUNK.

We all had a terrible night's sleep, and when we woke in the morning, we realized it wasn't just US that stunk. It was everything inside the camper, too.

So we emptied the whole thing out. And it was pretty clear we were gonna have to throw almost everything away, especially our FOOD.

Mom gave me money and sent me up to the camp store to get the deskunking supplies and some groceries. But on my way up there, I could tell something wasn't RIGHT.

By the time I got to the store, all the food was GONE, and the shelves were practically bare. I was lucky there was still some hydrogen peroxide and baking soda left, because if I'd got there a few minutes later, somebody probably would've scooped them up, too.

I tried to ask someone what was happening, but I guess the ketchup and mustard weren't doing their job covering up the skunk smell.

After I paid for my stuff and left, I ran into DooDoo, who didn't seem to even NOTICE the way I smelled.

He told me the reason people were acting crazy was because last night a bolt of lightning struck the bridge leading to the campground, and one section of the bridge was totally DESTROYED.

He said the truck that brings supplies couldn't get onto the property, which explained why everyone was snapping up everything at the store.

But now I was the one who was panicking. Because if nobody could get IN to camp, that meant nobody could get OUT, either.

I ran back to tell Mom and Dad what was going on. But by then our neighbors had woken up, and apparently they weren't crazy about the skunk smell.

I filled Mom and Dad in on the bridge situation. Mom said the most important thing was that we didn't PANIC, because that never helps. And she said that what we should be focused on right now was getting rid of this ODOR.

The deskunking instructions said to pour the baking soda and hydrogen peroxide in a hot bath, but it's not like there were a bunch of bathtubs on the campground. So we used the next best thing. And it turns out dogs don't like the smell of skunk, either.

We must've soaked in the hot tub for an hour. But in the time it took to scrub our bodies and our clothes clean, things at camp had gone TOTALLY off the rails.

It started with the WATER. When the camp store ran out of water bottles, people used the spigot by the main lodge to fill up their containers.

Some people took more than they needed, though, and the well ran DRY.

So then people got water from wherever they could FIND it.

Things got REALLY ugly when people ran out of the coins they needed to operate the showers.

So now quarters were like GOLD, and I heard about a woman who sold her wedding ring for seventy-five cents.

Some people got frustrated they couldn't get their hands on any coins, so they raided the ARCADE.

People hit the laundromat next. And I knew this whole PLACE was gonna stink after everybody ran out of clean clothes.

Eventually someone got the bright idea to get the water directly from the plastic tank above the bathhouse.

The tank fell off the roof and rolled down the hill, where it leaked out half the water before coming to a stop at one of the horseshoe pits. Then the OTHER half emptied out into the sand.

Now people were REALLY freaking out and tried to save what they could. But the horseshoe pit turned into QUICKSAND, and a few people actually had to be RESCUED.

Around dinnertime, everyone started getting HUNGRY. Some people had enough food to last them a few days, but everyone else was counting on getting their groceries from the camp store.

So things started to get a little CRAZY. A bunch of people raided the snack shack, and one person stole a giant bag of food from the pet-friendly area.

The animals must've got the sense that things were getting out of control, so they banded TOGETHER.

And when one of our neighbors fired up their grill to cook some hamburgers, a pack of dogs made its move.

A few people ate the leftover hot dogs from the pool party, and the teenagers from the hill salvaged some of their slingshot ammunition down at the field.

I was more NERVOUS than hungry. People do crazy things when they're desperate, and I had no idea how bad things would get. So I kept my shirt off to show everyone that I didn't have a lot of MEAT on me.

The other thing I was worried about was the WEATHER. Dad's phone said another storm was coming tonight, and that was the LAST thing this place needed.

Emergency Alert

Flash flood warning in effect until 9:00 a.m.

Mom said everyone was OVERREACTING, and that by morning someone would repair the bridge and everything would go back to normal.

But when night fell, things at the campground got a whole lot WORSE. And when one of the deluxe campers got tipped over by people who thought they were hoarding canned food and toilet paper inside, Mom finally admitted things were SERIOUS.

Now we ALL wanted to get out of this place, but nobody could figure out HOW. And that's when I thought of the STREAM.

I remembered there was one part that was really SHALLOW, and I said we might be able to drive the camper over the rocks and get to the other side.

I thought everyone would say my idea was stupid, but when a camper two doors down got tipped over, we were ready to try just about ANYTHING.

We didn't wanna call a lot of attention to ourselves by turning on the engine, so we pushed the camper off the pad and down the hill. And once we got it going, the camper really started MOVING.

The only problem was we forgot to detach the sewer line before we got rolling, and it made a giant MESS on our site.

But there was no going back now, and when the camper started picking up speed, we all climbed on board.

We coasted to the bottom of the hill, where the lake emptied into the stream. And when we were far enough away from everyone else, it seemed safe to start the engine.

We kept the headlights off because we didn't want anyone to SEE us. But that made it tricky to find the shallow spot in the stream.

By now it had started to RAIN, and it was coming down pretty hard. But when we turned the headlights back on, I finally found the place where the stream was shallow.

Dad put his foot on the accelerator. We edged out slowly, and for a minute it looked like we were gonna be able to make it all the way across.

But once we got to the middle of the stream, there was an awful sound, and the camper ground to a halt.

We were stuck on a giant ROCK, and something got knocked loose from the bottom of the camper. I'm not an expert on cars or anything, but whatever that thing was, it looked like it was pretty IMPORTANT.

But it turned out that was the LEAST of our problems. The rain was getting a lot HEAVIER, and all of a sudden the stream wasn't so SHALLOW anymore.

Now our sewage hookup was UNDERWATER, and it didn't take long for the system to back up.

The mess in the bathroom overflowed into the main living area, and we scrambled to keep off the floor. We knew we couldn't stay inside the camper, so we tried to get OUT. But by now the water in the stream was moving so fast, it wasn't SAFE to leave.

The camper was filling up with water, and we had to climb even HIGHER. Rodrick pulled himself onto the roof first, and then helped the REST of us up to safety.

But once we were all on the roof, the camper started to TURN.

By now the stream was overflowing, and the camper lifted free from the rock it was stuck on. Five seconds later, we were drifting downstream.

We were headed right for that BRIDGE. And if we had stayed where we were on the roof, that thing would have taken our HEADS off.

That's when I noticed that some of the seat cushions from the kitchen had floated outside the side door. I jumped first, and everyone else followed my lead.

The only person who didn't jump was MANNY. He had climbed back down into the camper and was sitting in the DRIVER'S seat.

The rest of us were freaking out, because the camper was about to hit the BRIDGE.

But at the last second, Manny pulled the wheel hard to the right, and the camper started to TURN. And when it reached the bridge, the camper snapped into place like a puzzle piece.

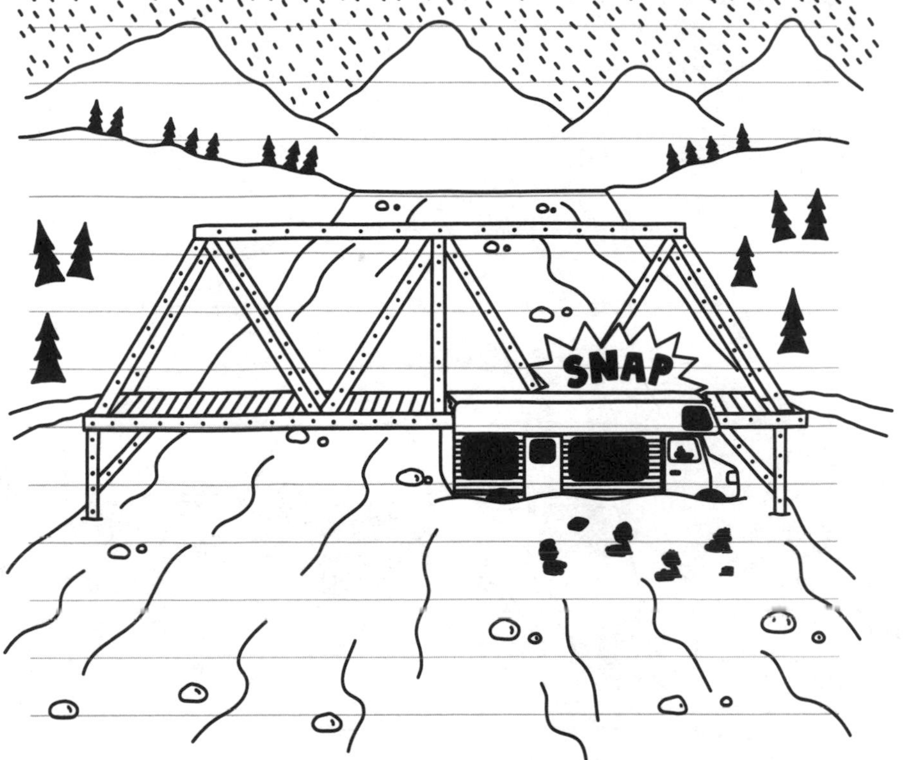

Manny wasn't FINISHED, though. He grabbed something out of the glove compartment, then he shot off the flare gun for the second time this trip.

Even though it was still raining hard, the flare lit up the sky. A few minutes later, we saw headlights coming our way. At first I thought people were coming to RESCUE us. But when they got to the bridge, they just kept GOING.

It took a full HOUR for all the vehicles to cross to the other side.

And when the very last motorcyle drove over the bridge, the only thing we could hear was the rain.

Saturday

After the campground emptied out, we were the only ones LEFT. With all the people gone, we were finally able to enjoy ourselves. And for once, Campers' Eden lived up to its NAME.

So all it took for this place to turn into paradise was for everyone else to LEAVE.

Two days after the storm, the delivery truck came back to supply the camp store. And that night, we ate like KINGS.

We had the whole lake to ourselves, too. And since the water was nice and deep, we actually had FUN.

I don't wanna be corny or anything, but we actually DID make a few happy memories during our stay.

But I just wanna point out that I was right, because it took a miracle for it to happen.

I'm not sure we needed to go through all that DRAMA, though. So maybe the next time we do something as a family, we can stick with something BORING, like mini golf.

I'm really looking forward to telling Rowley about my vacation when I get back. But I'll probably leave out the parts that weren't so great.

And I might change a few other details here and there, because you should never let the truth get in the way of a good story.

ACKNOWLEDGMENTS

Thanks to all the fans who have made my dream of becoming a cartoonist a reality. Thanks to my wife, Julie, and to my whole family for cheering me on through deadlines.

Thanks to Charlie Kochman for being my partner in crime for all these years, and for your dedication to making great books. Thanks to everyone at Abrams, including Michael Jacobs, Andrew Smith, Hallie Patterson, Melanie Chang, Kim Lauber, Mary O'Mara, Alison Gervais, and Elisa Gonzalez. Thanks also to Susan Van Metre and Steve Roman.

Thanks to the Wimpy Kid team (Shae'Vana!): Shaelyn Germain, Vanessa Jedrej, and Anna Cesary. Thanks to Deb Sundin, Kym Havens, and the incredible team at An Unlikely Story.

Thanks to Rich Carr and Andrea Lucey for your outstanding support. Thanks to Paul Sennott for your expert advice. Thanks to Sylvie Rabineau and Keith Fleer for everything you do for me. Thanks to Roland Poindexter, Ralph Millero, Vanessa Morrison, and Michael Musgrave for bringing fresh excitement to the Wimpy World.

As always, thanks to Jess Brallier for your friendship and support.

ABOUT THE AUTHOR

Jeff Kinney is a #1 *New York Times* bestselling author and a six-time Nickelodeon Kids' Choice Award winner for Favorite Book. Jeff has been named one of *Time* magazine's 100 Most Influential People in the World. He is also the creator of Poptropica, which was named one of *Time*'s 50 Best Websites. He spent his childhood in the Washington, D.C., area and moved to New England in 1995. Jeff lives with his wife and two sons in Massachusetts, where they own a bookstore, An Unlikely Story.